BEARCUB BIOS

ACTOR AND SOCIAL ACTIVIST

by Rachel Rose

Consultant: Beth Gambro
Reading Specialist, Yorkville, Illinois

BEARPORT
PUBLISHING

Minneapolis, Minnesota

Teaching Tips

BEFORE READING

- Discuss what a biography is. What kinds of things might a biography tell a reader?

- Look through the glossary together. Read and discuss the words.

- Go on a picture walk, looking through the pictures to discuss vocabulary and make predictions about the text.

DURING READING

- Encourage readers to point to each word as it is read. Stop occasionally to ask readers to point to a specific word in the text.

- If a reader encounters an unknown word, ask them to look at the rest of the page. Are there any clues to help them understand?

AFTER READING

- Check for understanding.
  - Where was Yara Shahidi born?
  - What does she do?
  - What does she care about?

- Ask the readers to think deeper.
  - If you met Yara, what question would you like to ask her? Why?

Credits:

Cover and title page, © Featureflash Photo Agency/Shutterstock and © Ververidis Vasilis/Shutterstock; 3, © Ga Fullner/Shutterstock; 5, © Paul Archuleta/Getty Images; 7, © Eric McCandless/Getty Images; 8, © David Livingston/Getty Images; 11, © Patrick McMullan/Getty Images; 13, © Alberto E. Rodriguez/Getty Images; 14-15, © fizkes/Shutterstock; 16-17, © Paul Archuleta/Getty Images; 19, © Paul Morigi/Getty Images; 20, © Astrid Stawiarz/Getty Images; 22, © Ga Fullner/Shutterstock; 23TL, © lunamarina/Shutterstock; 23TC, © Riguar/Shutterstock; 23TR, © Everett Historical/Shutterstock; 23BL, © vchal/Shutterstock; 23BC, © adamkaz/iStock; and 23BR, and © Henrik5000/iStock.

Library of Congress Cataloging-in-Publication Data

Names: Rose, Rachel, 1968– author. Title: Yara Shahidi : actor and social activist / by Rachel Rose. Description: Bearcub books. | Minneapolis, Minnesota : Bearport Publishing Company, [2021] | Series: Bearcub bios | Includes bibliographical references and index. Identifiers: LCCN 2020000585 (print) | LCCN 2020000586 (ebook) | ISBN 9781642809848 (library binding) | ISBN 9781642809954 (paperback) | ISBN 9781647470067 (ebook) Subjects: LCSH: Shahidi, Yara—Juvenile literature. | Actresses—United States—Biography—Juvenile literature. | Political activists—United States—Biography—Juvenile literature. Classification: LCC PN2287.S357 R67 2021 (print) | LCC PN2287.S357 (ebook) | DDC 791.4502/8092 [B]—dc23 LC record available at https://lccn.loc.gov/2020000585LC ebook record available at https://lccn.loc.gov/2020000586

For more information, write to Bearport Publishing, 5357 Penn Avenue South, Minneapolis, MN 55419.

Printed in the United States of America.

Contents

Birthday Girl

February 10, 2018, was a big day.

It was Yara Shahidi's 18th birthday.

Now, she could **vote**.

She could help pick who is in charge.

5

Yara's Life

Yara was born in Minnesota.

She grew up in California.

Her family moved there when she was four.

Yara's mother is an actor.

Yara wanted to act, too.

She was in **commercials** when she was six!

Yara got a big acting job when she was nine.

She was in a movie!

She played a girl named Olivia.

Olivia had a **magic** blanket.

Later, Yara also acted in TV shows.

She played a girl named Zoey.

Yara with others from her TV show

13

Yara cares about the world.

In high school, she started a club.

Students in the club talked about problems.

They wanted to make the world better.

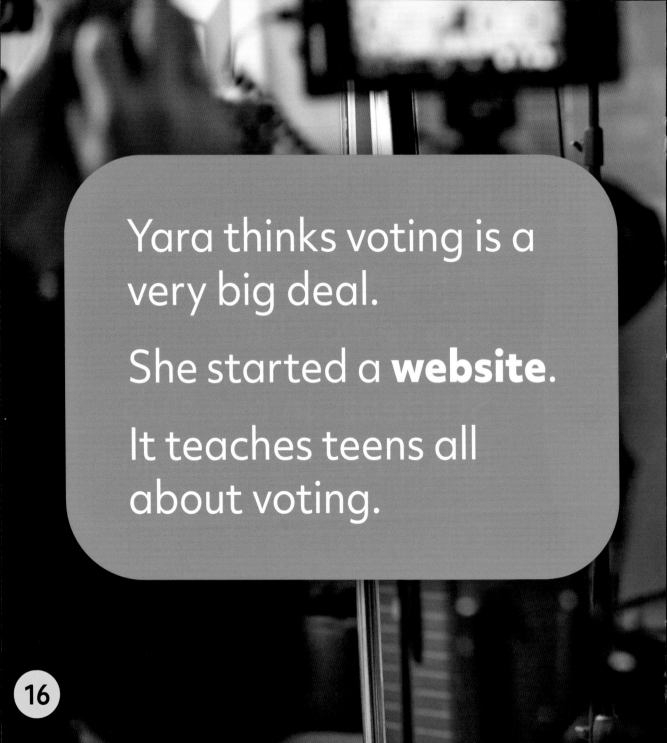

Yara thinks voting is a very big deal.

She started a **website**.

It teaches teens all about voting.

Yara is friends with Michelle Obama.

They both care about girls going to good schools.

They speak about it together.

Now, Yara is in college.

She still acts.

And she still talks about world problems.

She stands up for young people.

Did You Know?

Born: February 10, 2000

Family: Keri (mother), Afshin (father), Sayeed (brother), Ehsan (brother)

When she was a kid: Her favorite classes in school were **history** and math.

Special fact: The name Yara means someone who is close to your heart.

Yara says: "I want to help **effect** change."

Life Connections

Yara wants to make the world a better place. What do you care about? Are there things that you would like to change?

Glossary

commercials ads on TV

effect what happens because of something

history the subject where you learn about what happened in the past

magic something with special powers

vote to make a choice about someone or something

website a place on the internet that has pictures and information

Index

Read More

Waxman, Laura Hamilton. *Cool Kid Actors (Lightning Bolt Books Kids in Charge!).* Minneapolis: Lerner Publications (2020).

Hudd, Emily. *Yara Shahidi (Influential People).* North Mankato, MN: Capstone Press (2020).

Learn More Online

1. Go to **www.factsurfer.com**
2. Enter "**Yara Shahidi**" into the search box.
3. Click on the cover of this book to see a list of websites.

About the Author

Rachel Rose writes books for children and teaches yoga. She lives in San Francisco with her husband and her dog, Sandy.